IFEOMA ONYEFULU was brought up in eastern Nigeria.
Her internationally-acclaimed photography has been described
by *Books for Keeps* as *"stepping from a darkened room straight into noon sunshine"*.

Her first book, *A is for Africa,* was praised by *Publishers Weekly* for its
"incisive, sophisticated view of her homeland's rich heritage". *One Big Family* was
chosen both as a Notable Book for Children by the American Library Association,
and also as a Notable Children's Trade Book in the Field of Social Studies
by the National Council for Social Studies and the U.S. Children's Book Council.
In 2005, *Here Comes Our Bride!* – the third in her African ceremonies series
which also includes *Welcome Dede!* and *Saying Goodbye* – won the
U.S. Children's Africana Book Award: Best Book for Young Children.

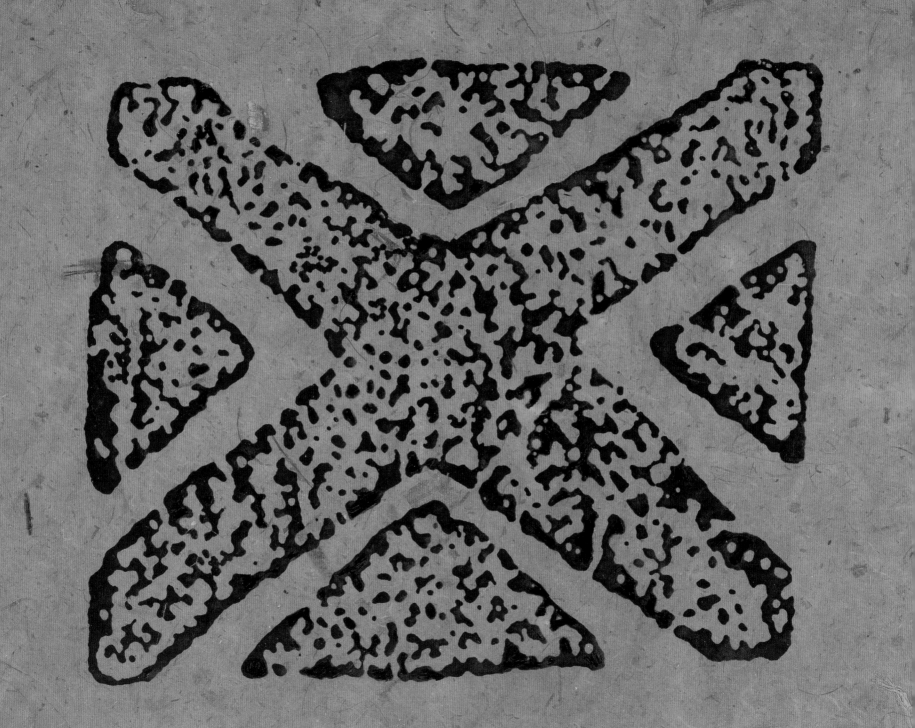

To the people of Awkuzu and Onitsha, and to Emeka,
for being a wonderful travelling companion

Textile designs for cover and endpapers by Chinye Onyefulu

One Big Family copyright © Frances Lincoln Limited 1996
Text and photographs copyright © Ifeoma Onyefulu 1996

First published in Great Britain in 1996 by
Frances Lincoln Children's Books, 4 Torriano Mews,
Torriano Avenue, London NW5 2RZ
www.franceslincoln.com

This paperback edition first published in Great Britain and the USA in 2006

British Library Cataloguing in Publication Data available on request

ISBN 10: 1-84507-686-9
ISBN 13: 978-1-84507-686-3

Printed in China

1 3 5 7 9 8 6 4 2

ONE BIG FAMILY

Sharing life in an African village

Ifeoma Onyefulu

F

FRANCES LINCOLN
CHILDREN'S BOOKS

This book is about sharing - about celebrating together and helping one another.

In my part of Africa, Igboland in Eastern Nigeria, one important way people do this is through their *ogbo* or age-group. Many African villages have chiefs, kings and queens or councils of elders, but everyone is expected to contribute to the day-to-day life of the village - and the older the person, the more duties his or her *ogbo* carries out. *Ogbo* exists alongside the family unit, but it goes beyond extended family ties and provides a helping hand in times of difficulty.

In some villages, all children born in a given year are grouped into one *ogbo*; in others, all the children born in a two, three, four or five-year period share an *ogbo*.

Some people choose not to belong to an *ogbo*. Others, like myself, continue to stay in touch with their *ogbo* even when they move away to the city, bringing new ideas to meetings and taking away with them the warmth and friendship *ogbo* offers.

When I took these photographs, I asked the old men and women I know how long *ogbo* has been going on. "As long as there have been births, *ogbo* has been in existence," was their reply. And as long as children are born, there will always be *ogbo*.

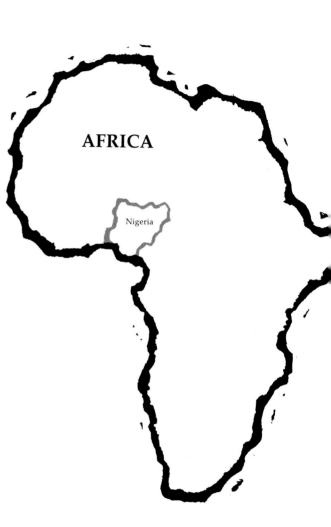

AFRICA

Nigeria

Hello!

My name is Obioma (pronounced o-bee-Oma). I live in a village called Awkuzu (aw-KOO-zoo), and I belong to an *ogbo* (or-BO) or age-group.

In Awkuzu, every child belongs to an *ogbo*, together with all the other children born within a five-year period. Fat or thin, rich or poor, it does not matter. Everyone has a friend; no one is born alone. We belong to our *ogbo* all through our lives. All the *ogbo* help to run the village, and on special occasions they come together to share each other's joys and sorrows.

Let me tell you about the members of my family and each of their *ogbo*.

My big brother is called Ifeanyi (ee-FAY-ny-ee). I like him very much and we often play together.

Ifeanyi is ten years old, the age when children start helping in the village, so his *ogbo* already has a job. It helps to keep the village *ilo* (ee-LO) clean. This is a big open space where children can play safely and where important events like festivals and village meetings take place.

Ifeanyi's job is to sound the *ogene* (o-gay-nee), to let everyone in his *ogbo* know that it is their turn to sweep. He enjoys his work so much that he goes on playing long after the children have all arrived with their brooms. Here they are - with everyone trying to be the first to finish!

My mother is known as Mama Ifeanyi, after Ifeanyi her eldest son. She belongs to an *ogbo* called Obinwanne (o-BEEN-war-nay), which means "kind heart of a sister or brother". Obinwanne do lots of jobs in the village. Here they are, sweeping dead leaves and grasses from the stream. They do this twice a month, leaving the water clean so that we can drink and wash in it.

Obinwanne also take turns keeping watch over people's farms. If an animal strays and eats someone's vegetable crop, they report it to the chiefs, who then ask the animal's owner to pay for the damage.

Like every other *ogbo*, Obinwanne help one another, too. When one of them is ill, they all bring money and food to help the person get well.

Best of all, Obinwanne sing sweet songs and dance at special events. They have won competitions for our village. Here is my mother smiling and holding her *ishaka* (ee-shar-ka), a beautiful musical instrument which she loves to play.

Everyone calls my father Papa Ifeanyi. He is forty years old and his *ogbo* is called Igwebike (ee-WAY-BEE-kay), meaning "together-is-strength". Igwebike really do stay together and are very strong too! This year they are building the first nursery school in the village.

Ogbo make all their decisions by voting. Igwebike even vote on the colours and styles of the costumes they will wear on special occasions to distinguish them from other *ogbo*.

My father loves dancing and showing off his nice clothes. Here he is holding a fan in one hand and a feather in the other to show that he is the leader of his *ogbo*.

Igwebike chose the wisest person in the group to be their leader. I think they made the right choice!

Amuoku (ah-moo-O-KOO), which means "lighting a fire", is the name of my uncle Chike's (ChEE-kays) *ogbo*. He is twenty years old and his *ogbo* has just chosen its name.

Uncle Chike works in the city, but he was there when his *ogbo* chose its name. He comes back most weekends to visit us and to help his *ogbo*. I like him because he brings me biscuits from the city. My mother says he also brings along new ideas to help make Amuoku's work quicker and easier.

If anyone wants a house built, but cannot afford to pay, Amuoku will build it without asking the person to pay anything. The owner of the new house says "thank you" by cooking a nice meal for them.

Last year, Amuoku helped to build roads and market stalls for my village. My father says that to do all this they must have fire in their belly. I too think they are young and strong!

At the end of every year, Amuoku present masquerades to celebrate the new planting season. Here are some of them with an animal masquerade. Masquerades are costumes and masks which are made to honour the spirits of our ancestors, and are brought out only on special occasions. Artists spend months and months making them.

And here is my uncle Chike enjoying himself at the festival.

Last week was a very special occasion: my favourite auntie was made a chief. It was my village's way of thanking her for all the help she has given to sick people, especially to children. Being made a chief was a great honour for her because she is only thirty years old. Her name is Ngozi (un-GO-zee), but even though she is a chief, I still call her "Auntie".

Here she is, surrounded by beautiful fabrics and holding her chief's horse-tail, which she will now take with her wherever she goes.

M y auntie invited all the men and women in her *ogbo*, Obinwanne (which is also my mother's *ogbo*), to share the joy of this special occasion. My family were so happy for her that they invited their *ogbo* along too! Everybody danced and danced and ate and ate.

Here you can see the women dancing in a separate group. Sometimes they prefer to stay separate from the men in their *ogbo*, although they still share the same *ogbo* name and celebrate festivals together.

This is my grandfather, whom we call Nnam Ochie (nam-OH-chee-eh). He is 70 years old, and I like to look at all the lines on his face when he is telling us stories. His *ogbo* is called Asammanuboko (a-sam-anoo-BO-ko), which means "beauty".

My grandfather says that Asammanuboko chose their name when they were young and beautiful. Now they are old and wise - and that makes them beautiful, too!

Everyone listens to the wise words of Asammanuboko, for they are the village leaders. Each month the people in my village bring problems to them.

There are other *ogbo* even older than Asammanuboko. They are usually given the place of honour in the front seats during festivals, but they are too old to do much for the village - in fact, the younger *ogbo* often help them.

There are only a few Asammanuboko now. Some are not well enough to come to meetings any more, and some have gone to join our ancestors. One day, another *ogbo* will take the place of Asammanuboko as rulers of the village. But everyone hopes they still have many more years left to them.

When a very old person dies, his or her *ogbo* asks everyone who knew the person to the funeral to wish them a good journey to our ancestors. Although the dead person's relatives are sad, for everyone else this is a joyful time because, if someone has lived a long and happy life, we see their death as a reason to rejoice, not to grieve.

For several days before the burial, we celebrate the things that the dead person liked best. If, for example, they loved the sound of drums, their *ogbo* will bring out the drums to be played. On the day of the burial, their family, *ogbo* and friends each say their goodbyes aloud to the dead person before he or she is laid to rest.

After the burial, the *ogbo* of the dead person's family sing and dance to help the relatives in their sadness - which is what these children are doing.

I am six years old, and almost every day I meet one or two children who are in the same age group as me. We visit each other's houses and sometimes eat with our *ogbo* friends. In the evenings, we sit and listen to older members of our families telling folk tales.

I cannot wait to be a grown-up like my mother and do all the things her *ogbo* does. But right now, all we do is play. Here are the boys in my *ogbo* wearing painted boxes over their heads and pretending to be grown-up masqueraders. They dress up and chase the girls, just for fun!

I do not know how many there are in my *ogbo*, because my village is very big and we are still very small, so we do not yet have meetings. But grown-ups, especially my grandfather, sometimes point out other children in my group and tell me more about what it means to belong to an *ogbo*.

For me, belonging to an *ogbo* is very special - like belonging to one big family.